I0822596

Apples of Gold

…A Book of Godly Wisdom

Reno Omokri

Apples of Gold:
A Book of Godly Wisdom

Published by
The Mind of Christ Christian Center
Box 863
Brentwood, CA 94513

RevMedia Publishing
PO Box 5172
Kingwood, TX 77325
www.revmediapublishing.com

ISBN-13: 978-0-9981829-4-0
ISBN10 0-9981829-4-X
Printed in the United States of America

1 2 3 4 5 6 7 8 9 10 11 21 20 19 18 17 16 15 14

TABLE OF CONTENTS

DEDICATION

This book is dedicated to my dear mother, Mercy, who has recently turned 80. She taught me to love God and to love reading The Bible at age 6 and made sure I continued down the path that I am still on today at age 43.

Reno Omokri in a hand shake with Dr. Goodluck Ebele Jonathan President of Nigeria (2010-2015)

FOREWORD

This book, *Apples of Gold,* is a compilation of wisdom from the word of God and divine Inspiration from His Spirit. It is a book that will help the reader get wisdom and in the getting it will also help such persons get understanding. It deals with every area of life, including love, marriage, parenting, finances and many other institutions and situations that a person must go through from birth to death. I am so glad Reno allowed himself to be the vessel through whom this book came. And, let me say that I personally believe that no matter how intelligent a person is, their intelligence will take them to many high places but it will not be able to keep them there. The Father promoted Jesus and gave Him the highest Name not because of our Lord's intelligence, though He is the most intelligent. In Philippians chapter two and verses eight and nine, The Father revealed through Apostle Paul the reasons for which He gave Jesus a name above all names. Jesus is Loyal and Humble. These qualities are the same ones that I have found in this servant of God. Reno Omokri has shown loyalty and humility. To me, to his country, to the Body of Christ and to his friends and family.

He is looking up to Jesus and is painting his own life after the image of his Lord and mine.

When you read this book, you will appreciate the heart from which such humility and loyalty flow. You will appreciate a heart that is in love with God.

Dr. Goodluck Ebele Jonathan
President of Nigeria (2010-2015)

Reno Omokri, like the biblical Daniel, is a man of God and a man influential in politics. Of course, the public knows he is a very intelligent young man who has helped made great men greater, but what many people may not know is that he is an incredibly loyal person. He is the definition of loyalty and I do not exaggerate. He may take time to decide if he will be your friend or associate, but when he does elect to do so, he sticks to you closer than a brother. He will not just be for what you are for (as long as it is Godly), he will be for you. As a Presidential spokesman and newspaper columnist, he has proven his intelligence mettle, but in this book of wisdom called *Apples of Gold*, he had displayed wisdom that could only have been given him by his Creator.

—Senator Ben Murray-Bruce

INTRODUCTION

In Job 38:33 we read *'Do you know the laws of the universe? Can you use them to regulate the earth?'* (NLT)

Without knowing those universal laws or principles which regulate the earth we will not be able to fulfill our first charge from God-to be fruitful and have dominion on earth (Genesis 1:28).

This book is an attempt to bring you some of the most vital of those principles in language that is contemporary and that you can relate to. The title of this book comes from Proverbs 25:11 *'A word fitly spoken is like apples of gold in pictures of silver.'* (KJV).

We all need such apples so our conversation will always be full of grace, seasoned with salt, so we may know how to answer everyone. (Colossians 4:6). And the word conversation here is used not just in reference to oral conversation but also includes our behavior and daily pattern of life, our habits which in turn shape our destiny.

Proverbs 25:11 indicates that these apples of Gold will help frame our lives in silver frames. The implication of this is that when we understand Godly wisdom and apply it in our lives, we will end up with a life that is worth being recorded in history as an example to future generations. We will end up with a life of significance.

The future is merely consequence catching up to our words and actions of today. This book will help you influence and even create the future you desire by elucidating Godly and biblical principles which if you follow today you will be followed tomorrow.

Many people write about things that they know, which in itself is not something bad. But the wisdoms in this book are largely wisdoms that I have experiential knowledge of.

God is no respecter of persons. If they worked for me when I applied them, they will definitely work for you if you apply them too. God created man to be a co-creator with Him which is why Jesus told us in Mark 11:23 to speak to mountains in our lives. This book will give you the wisdom power to speak authoritatively to your mountains and get results. Lasting results!

It will also help you identify your life's purpose. Remember, no matter how many university degrees you have, if you do not know your life's purpose, you are no better than an illiterate and you may even be worse of because some illiterates know their lives purpose. A man who does not know his purpose is condemned to forever be an onlooker in his life instead of the main driver of a car going to a destination prearranged by God.

In Matthew 16:19 Jesus said *'I will give you the keys of the kingdom of heaven; whatever you bind on earth will be bound in heaven, and whatever you loose on earth will be loosed in heaven.'* (NIV)

Those keys are not physical keys. They are the principles of the kingdom. And note what Jesus said would happen when you know those keys. He said then *'whatever you bind on earth will be bound in heaven, and whatever you loose on earth will be loosed in heaven'*. What Jesus said here is exactly what was said in Job 38:33 *'Do you know the laws of the universe? Can you use them to regulate the earth?'*

You see, when you know the keys to the kingdom, the laws of the universe, you can use them to regulate the earth such that *'whatever you bind on earth will be bound in heaven, and whatever you loose on earth will be loosed in heaven'*. I cannot wait to hear all the great and mighty things God will do in your life as you read and apply these principles. Certainly, I can say that if you do apply these principles it is a given that the rest of your life will be the best of your life.

—B. Reno Omokri

Wednesday January 18, 2017
Brentwood, California

I. SPIRITUALITY

And thou shalt love the LORD thy God with all thine heart, and with all thy soul, and with all thy might.
DEUTERONOMY 6:5

Whatever you give priority focus to is your God. If you wake up and check your phone before your God then your god is your phone.

Have faith in God, but still prepare for emergencies. That is why God gave you wisdom. So you can plan, not so you can pray alone.

Instead of idolizing celebrities who do not know of your existence, worship only the God who gave you your existence.

You cannot curse your enemies and expect God to bless you. Your enemies are also God's kids. God does not love you more than them.

With God, It is better to have your heart right and your actions wrong than to have your actions right and your heart wrong.

Once you boast to others about the offering you gave to God, it stops being an offering and becomes an offending.

The greatest waste of money is to pay tithes in order to impress a pastor. Keep your tithe a tight secret between you and God.

One of the saddest things I see in Christianity are people who draw closer to pastors and equate it with drawing closer to God.

When Satan comes to afflict you, do not start crying 'why me', remember your relationship with God and say 'try me' instead.

Do not confuse being a Christian with trying to be nice. Nice folks focus on pleasing everyone. Christians focus on pleasing God.

Be suspicious of any Christianity whose end result is miracles, signs and wonder, rather than evangelism and dying to self.

The fool says there is no God since he cannot see Him but proceeds to log onto a Wi-Fi connection that he cannot see yet believes in.

Before showering pastors who prayed for you with money remember that your mother has been praying for you before you were born.

Satan has gone into the miracle business since he knows that is what attracts people instead of self-sacrifice and salvation.

The purpose of church is not to lead men to miracles and financial breakthrough. Even satan can do that. It is to lead men to God.

Driving your car on an empty tank destroys your engine and running your life with an empty prayer life destroys your destiny.

Being too busy to pray is like being too busy to breathe. It is the essential function that makes you able to enjoy your busyness.

People who dress powerfully know how to impress people, but those who pray powerfully know how to influence people.

Fools want to become great by using God for their purpose while wise men become great by surrendering to be used by God.

Do not compete with others. There are 7 billion people on earth. It will wear you out. Compete with the person you were yesterday.

Would Christianity have reached us if early believers focused on miracles and financial breakthroughs instead of evangelism?

The reason many people's prayers go unanswered is because they remember God when they are afraid and forget him when they are happy.

The more you meditate on God's word the less you will medicate on manmade medicine. Heal your mind and the body will follow.

Nobody likes a fair weather friend, including God. Do not wait until you need something to pray. Pray and thank God daily.

If we do not delete unforgiveness from our heart we can never download God's blessings into our life no matter how long we pray.

As shoe shines when you brush it with shoe polish, so will our lives shine when we brush it with the life polish called prayer.

Pray to God for what you want, but never tell him how He should do it. You can never have better know how Than God!

II. GOALS, SUCCESS & FAILURE

This book of the law shall not depart out of thy mouth; but thou shalt meditate therein day and night, that thou mayest observe to do according to all that is written therein: for then thou shalt make thy way prosperous and then thou shalt have good success.

JOSHUA 1:8

If you define success as having money, then even some thieves are successful. Success is actualizing your God given potential.

A man who cannot control appetite for food or women is a man who will not fulfill potential. Too much of anything leads to failure.

Dreams can come true but you have to come through with your plans for making them come true or they will remain just dreams.

When tempted to worry, convert the worry to planning. It takes the same effort but one is creative and the other is destructive.

Those who dress for success without working for it are like men who buy a Porsche and fail to fuel it. They are not going anywhere.

Overnight success only happens in movies. In real life what exists is overtime success. Success occurs over a period of time.

Find your purpose. Find your passion. Find yourself and find your life partner. If you find all four, success will find you.

Those who brag about success cannot grab it for long and those who grab success for long do not brag about it at all.

Do not do too many things at once. Multitasking does not multiply your focus. It dilutes focus. Do one thing excellently at a time.

Do not have too many goals. Be like a military strategist. They do not have many goals, but the few that they have are very clear.

You cannot get what you hate. If you hate successful people or you dislike rich folks, success and riches will forever elude you.

God asked us to develop patience so we can be patient with people but not so that we can be patient with failure.

If you love being promoted in life then you must love solving problems in life. Promotion is a reward for providing solutions.

God put inside you everything you need to be a resounding success. Your duty is to work out what God has worked into you.

No one owes you success. That is a debt you must pay to yourself. If you do not, it will remain unpaid until you leave this planet.

Never boast. Boasting is a symptom of low self-esteem. If you feel good about yourself you will not feel the need to brag.

FAILURE and SUCCESS are both 7 letter words that teach us that what we do with our 7 day week is the difference between them.

Success comes from deciding early what direction you want to go and only make friends with people going in the same direction.

Humility does not mean you should not aspire to be great. Jesus is Great yet humble. Do not confuse mediocrity for humility.

Opportunity is a knocker, not a builder. If you want opportunity to knock on your door, you must build the door yourself.

Many people are poor today because they are too proud to ask those who have been to success for directions on how to get there.

A goal is a four letter word that will take you from where you are to where you want to be. Without goals you are going nowhere.

The favorite day of the week for lazy men is tomorrow. They can achieve a lot of great things but they can only do it tomorrow.

If you want to matter in life, you must start by having manners. Good manners open more doors than good looks or good money.

Billionaires are not snobbish because they hang out with other billionaires. Your association determines your elevation in life.

The big break you are looking for in life can only be found in the small breaks you are ignoring while waiting for the big break.

It is your own perception of yourself, not others perception of you, that will determine your success or failure in life.

Do not whine when you lose. Instead learn why you lost and tomorrow while other losers are whining, you will be winning!

Blind men with vision will succeed before men who see yet have no vision. An eagle's vision is what makes it the greatest bird.

Do not be proud of the many university degrees that you have. Instead, be proud of what you have used those degrees to achieve.

If you spend the day watching TV and browsing Internet, you will go to bed dumber than when you got up. Read books to get smarter.

There are seven days in a week and none of them is named one of these days. Be specific with your plans or the plan will not manifest.

Do not ask for rain if you do not want mud or sugar if you will not like ants or success if you cannot stand haters. They're inseparable.

How you treat yourself sets standards of how others treat you. Dress well to be addressed well. Value yourself to be respected.

Be tied to your potential not your history. Stop talking about the good old days and start planning for the better coming days.

Everyone makes mistakes. The difference is that wise men focus on recovering from mistakes while fools focus on who to blame.

Refuse to live up to anyone's expectations. Success is knowing who God says you are and hastening to meet His expectation of you.

Never make the mistake of equating being busy with being productive. A gossip is very busy yet very unproductive and destructive.

Do not get jealous of those who are more successful than you. Instead, befriend them and learn to be as successful as them.

Man naturally respects success. Instead of chasing respect, just chase success. When you catch it, respect will come naturally.

Be tough on yourself and life will be easy for you. Be soft on yourself and life will be hard on you. The choice is yours.

The way you think has more impact on your chances of success than how you look or what degrees you have. Think positively!

Determination is not just mental. It has a visual component. Write down goals. Seeing them in writing gives you determination.

The world rotates silently. We just sleep and wake up in tomorrow. Do not make noise. Let haters sleep and wake up to your success.

Every year you upgrade your phone and your car, but leave your mind the same by not reading books to upgrade it. Why?

Exams are a test of memory not a test of intelligence. Read to pass your exam but do not think you are unintelligent if you fail.

Do not be UPSET with failure. Reverse the word. Instead of being upset, SETUP yourself for success using daily self-development.

Nobody stole your idea. In fact, it was not your idea. Ideas come from God and if you waste them He gives it to someone else.

Do not mock humble beginnings.
Look at the initial Head Quarters of
HP, Apple, Amazon and Google.

Your dreams and your visions are not manufactured products. They do not have an expiration date.

III. CRITICISM & REJECTION

When my father and my mother forsake me,
then the LORD will take me up.
PSALM 27:10

Haters do not deserve your hatred. Leave such negative emotions with them. Do not stop being positive to respond to negativity.

If you do not respond to a barking dog, it will bark till it loses its voice. If you do not react to a hater the same thing happens.

The reason people make heaven is because God forgives them. The reason our lives becomes heavenly is because we forgive people.

Why hold offense because somebody offended you? Hold forgiveness and let the offender hold his offense. It is too heavy to carry.

No friend should ever be made a confidante until he has gone through thick and thin with you and never wavered in his friendship.

The problem with looking down on people is that it prevents you from looking up to God from whom all blessings flow.

The best way to stop getting annoyed with what people say about you is to start getting overjoyed by what God says about you.

Never look down on others and act superior to them simply because their sins have been exposed and yours remain a secret.

Do not let people's opinions about you change the fact about you. They may opine that you are useless. The fact is you are not.

Do not reduce your happiness because people are irritated by it. Does the sun stop shining because people squint at it?

Be glad that God not people have the final say or they would have finished you before God has finished with you.

Do not hate haters back. If a poisonous snake bites you and you bite it back all you are doing is collecting more poison.

It is always better to please God and let the world judge you than to please the world and let God judge you.

The best response to your haters is to transcend them in every way. Let their head ache from looking up to point at you.

Even if you mix salt with sugar, ants will only be attracted to the sugar. That is why haters leave others and focus on you.

A gossip is no one's friend. They thrill you but they also kill you. They will fascinate you but will also assassinate you.

You cannot be great if you fall apart because haters do not like you. Great people are used to haters not liking them.

Winners practice the discipline of managing their emotion. Haters practice the indiscipline of being managed by their emotions.

While haters know how to win an argument, winners know how to win in life. Instead of quarreling they focus on their calling.

Winners pursue 'betterness' by regularly improving themselves. Haters pursue bitterness by always comparing themselves to others.

Only befriend people who focus on self-development because those who do not develop themselves are experts at destroying others.

Everything happens for a reason. Without people who treated you wrong, you would not have had the experiences that made you strong.

The most unproductive venture is trying to please a hater. Just accept that not everybody will be glad when you are prospering.

When God wants to help you build your house, He allows enemies throw stones at you so you can gather them and build the house.

It is foolish to recognize the faults in others but not recognize that what you see in others exists much more in you.

When you call anyone ugly its God their Creator you insult. Critique people's character. They control that but not their looks.

Failures will call your success good luck and their failure an accident. They call your preparation hustle and their laziness faith.

The sweetness of any sugar that does not attract ants is in doubt and the success of men that do not have haters is in doubt.

Do not blame all the bad things that happen to you on haters. Some times it is just a case of reaping the evil you did yesterday.

Never lose your peace when you discover that someone hates you. It is not you that has the problem. It is them that have a problem.

No matter the label others give you; bully, bigot or racist, label yourself winner. Your self-label is what manifests in reality.

Haters will hate you just because of who you are. If you change who you are to please them they will hate you for being unstable.

Blow your own trumpet because if you do not blow it your enemies will blow it for you and you will not like the sound they make.

No matter what haters say about you, never react, just continue shining. The brilliance of your shine will overwhelm all hate.

When you notice someone flattering you, instead of smiling, be on alert. A hunter only uses bait when he wants to catch prey.

When you admit your flaws openly and immediately, you deprive your enemy of the ability of using them against you.

The only explanation you owe critics is to succeed when they expect you to fail. Your success will explain why they are wrong.

No matter how much you explain to them, your enemies will not believe you. Even before you explain, your friends have believed you.

Be careful who you confide in. Most foes were once friends and would not have had weapons against us if we had not confided in them.

Some people cause their own heartbreak because they confuse somebody who was curious about them for a confidante.

IV. LIFE, ATTITUDE & FRIENDSHIPS

For the commandment is a lamp; and the law is light; and reproofs of instruction are the way of life
PROVERBS 6:23

Many who think an hour is too long to spend praying tend not to think an hour is too long to spend watching TV.

Mature people do not wake up in the morning and gauge how they are feeling. They wake up and tell themselves how to feel.

It is foolish to think you can gain favor by badmouthing others to your boss. The best way to get favor is to always speak well of others.

Everyone goes to toilet like you, sweats like you and bleeds like you. No matter what position he holds, never worship a man.

Avoid talking when you are in a bad mood for the simple fact that moods come and go but words spoken are recorded in history.

Satan is always pleased when you get more religious as long as the religiosity leads to judgment over others instead of love.

Genius is the ability to simplify the complex, like Jesus did, not the ability to use big grammar to complicate simple things.

If you do not identify your purpose and pursue it others will think you are dull because you cannot fulfill their purpose for you.

The storms of your life will make you appreciate the difference between those who play with you and those who pray with you.

Watch how your friends treat people like gatemen or waiters. That is how they will treat you when they no longer benefit from you.

We can tell a lot about a man by watching him eat. Great men control their appetite. Weak men are controlled by their appetite.

Your location will not change your person. A butterfly that moves to America will not become a bird. It remains a relocated butterfly.

See good in bad situations. When it rains see rainbows. When it is dark see the stars. When in adversity, identify true friends.

Foolish people have multiple sources for their gossip while those they gossip about have multiple sources for their wealth.

If you have ever tried to change your own self then you will appreciate the wisdom in not trying to change others.

Never trust anybody that bad mouths his family member to you. If they can drink blood, they can certainly drink water.

There is nobody that is more beautiful THAN you because God made you beautiful AS you. So stop comparing yourself to others.

Nobody has a good or bad life. Everybody gets a life from God. It is you and I that make it good or bad not God or other people.

Everyone puts on a mask including you, therefore, never say you know anyone until the mask falls and you have seen them angry.

To have influence over people, cultivate the practice of making them leave your presence happier than when they came to you.

Do not hang out with people who you do not want to end up like. We become like our friends and our friends become like us.

Wisdom is ability to differentiate between things God has given you power to change and those He has given power to change you.

In life, education never ends. There is nothing like an educated man. There is only a man being educated. Life is education.

Even if you cannot afford big things yet because they are expensive at least you can afford to think big because thinking is free.

Whether you like it or not, you are growing older. The only choice you have in the matter is whether you will also grow wiser.

Tread with care. Women are the only legal gateway between the spiritual and physical. Do not make them angry enough to curse you.

The most visible sign of an immature and irresponsible person is complaining about things that are within your power to change.

Your life will not go forward if your mind is in reverse. Stop focusing on the past and you will be amazed the progress you will make.

The best medicines on earth are: Love, Forgiveness and Gratitude The worst poison on earth are: Hatred, Malice and Bitterness.

Those too busy to pray when they wake up are like dull knives with no time to be sharpened because they're too busy cutting.

Thank God for big problems. If God had not allowed you to have big problems, how would you have grown bigger than them?

The job of a friend is not to always agree with you. That is the job of your shadow. A friend disagrees with you when wrong.

Life is too short to tolerate a minute with those who kill your joy. If a friend terminates your joy, terminate the friendship.

Winning arguments at the cost of losing peace of mind is foolish. Let fools win their argument. Win your peace.

When you are optimistic, you optimize the gifts God gave you. When you are pessimistic, you minimize the talents God gave you.

Those who use anger to lash out at others misunderstand its purpose. Anger is meant to fuel your accomplishments not your rage.

Tie your sense of self-esteem to the fact that God loves you and you will not be too moved by praise or too shaken by criticism.

It is not possible to have low self-esteem when you read Psalm 139:14 and realize you are fearfully and wonderfully made.

Good Day + Bad Attitude = Bad Day
Bad Day + Good Attitude = Good Day.
Attitude is the quality that makes a day good or bad!

You only have a choice on actions you take, but you do not have a choice on its consequences, so use your power of choice wisely.

If thoughts were expensive you would be forgiven for thinking small but since they are free, there is no reason not to think big.

If we see life as a competition we have lots of enemies but if we see it as a journey we go through it with lots of friends.

What you pray for others is like a boomerang. It may hit them, but without fail it WILL always return to hit you back.

Avoid people without self-control because those who do not have self-control always want to control others.

A bad attitude is like bad body odor. If you do not do something about it even people that like you will begin to avoid you.

Do not waste time regretting missed opportunity. By wasting time regretting you are wasting other opportunities.

The most expensive things in life do not cost money. They cost peace of mind. Whatever affects your peace of mind is too costly.

Roses come with thorns, rain comes with mud, sugar always attracts ants and success always comes with haters. That is life.

The greatest waste of life is to grow older without growing wiser. A long life should be evidenced by wisdom not gray hair.

Have the largeness of heart to forgive friends who stabbed you in the back and the wisdom not to turn your back on them again.

Mature people forgive offenders, immature ones refuse to forgive and foolish people forget offenders who then offend them again.

During meetings, note those who badmouth those who did not attend because they will do same to you at any meeting you do not attend.

Real leaders do not blame. They correct what went wrong and prevent it from reoccurring. Blaming signifies helplessness.

Our minds are designed to be active. If we do not purposely entertain positive thoughts it will automatically host negative ones.

Do not wait to see what happens to you before deciding if today is a good day. If there is oxygen and you can breathe it is a good day.

A woman who will not expose her money publicly yet exposes her body publicly is saying that money is more valuable than her body.

When you fail, do not let anyone convince you that it is God's will. God created winners not losers. Keep at it until you win.

Keys to success: Do not keep malice, keep calm. Do not take offense, take initiative. Do not nurse grudges, nurse friendships.

Feed your intelligence, not your emotion. Read books to get more intelligent. Watch reality TV and you get more dramatic.

Confidence is the secret that makes people listen to us. Empathy is the reason they talk to us and wisdom is having both.

When you make another person too important to your own life they tend to make you less important in their life. Go for balance.

The future that awaits you is the consequence of your actions. So create beautiful actions because you will reap them in future.

Make sure your age is not the only proof that you have lived a long life. Let your wisdom also prove that you have lived for long.

If you do not taste it, you can mistake salt for sugar and if you do not test it, you can mistake arrogance for confidence.

Treat time like you treat money. Do not invest it on things and people that will not yield a positive return on your investments.

Do not try to prove how wise you are by saying wise words. Better to prove your wisdom by displaying wise choices and actions.

The power it takes to get angry is the same one it takes to remain calm. It is not a matter of strength. It is a matter of choice.

To know if anyone is loyal to you, withdraw benefit they enjoy from you. If loyalty fades then they were loyal to the benefits.

It is so ironic that those who do not have faith in God because they cannot see him have anxiety for tomorrow that they have not seen.

No matter what degree, status or experience they have, never let anyone's opinion of you determine your estimation of yourself.

Do not wait for your life to become perfect before you become happy. Instead become happy and your life will be perfect.

The more you try to impress people, the more depressed you will be because people do not get impressed by an impresser.

Use smartphones smartly. If they prevent you from spending time with loved ones, the phone may be smart but you are foolish.

Ten years from now what will matter will not be your designer clothes or your luxury car but what you learnt and how you used it.

An overinflated ego is poison to the soul. It makes a fool think he is wise and a ridiculous person think he is well respected.

Watching TV makes us more entertained than we were before watching. Reading books makes us smarter than we were before reading.

If you want your words to carry weight, do not speak because you want to say something. Speak because you have something to say.

Tears do not move satan. If you really want to make him miserable, maintain your smile no matter what trouble he brings your way.

The problem with most people is that they think education only happens in class rooms so they stop learning once out of school.

A butterfly is more beautiful than a bee but it cannot produce something as sweet as honey. We are all gifted in unique ways.

Only fools believe that good things come to those who wait. If good things do not come to you, my brother/sister, go to them!

Attitude is a language no one can understand. If you have an issue with somebody tell them. Do not speak to them using attitude.

Your head was not designed to store up a list of all those who have wronged you. Your head was designed to process ideas.

As we develop photos from negatives, so do our lives develop from our thoughts. Negative thoughts equals negative life.

Focus on yesterday and see regret, focus on tomorrow and see anxiety, focus on today and see opportunity.

V. ENTREPRENEURSHIP & FINANCE

Wilt thou set thine eyes upon that which is not? for riches certainly make themselves wings; they fly away as an eagle toward heaven.
PROVERBS 23:5

If you do not have contentment, no amount of wealth will make you feel rich. But if you have it, nothing will make you feel poor.

You may not get poor by saving your money, but you will certainly never get rich that way. Only wise investments bring riches.

Prepare your kids to be millionaire adults by giving them chores and paying them for it then teach them to invest their money.

Let your focus be on building your own wealth rather than on waiting to inherit your parents' wealth.

Do not compete with your neighbor. You do not know how he makes his money. It could be stealing. It could be debt. Run your race.

Inflation grows faster than interest rates so it makes no sense to save for the future. Instead, invest money for the future.

You cannot help the poor by taking money from the rich to give to them. Instead, take wisdom from the rich and give to the poor.

What you learn in school may help secure a high paying job. What you learn in life will help you create a high paying business.

Train yourself to be excited when you invest money instead of when you spend it and you will be a millionaire in the making.

Being rich is a mentality. If you take money away from someone with abundance mentality, his thinking will make it come back again.

Do not try to fit in if God has called you to stand out. Being the odd man is not bad. Billionaires are different from the crowd.

It is a mistake to call a poor man humble. Yes, he has been humbled. But to know if his humility is real, test him with wealth.

One of the few things money cannot buy is life, so do not risk your life to make it. Wealth without health is worse than poverty.

Your state of mind determines your status in life. Good thoughts will give you a great life better and faster than good money.

Your net worth grows if your intellect grows. Read and apply self-development books and your income will automatically develop.

Money runs from people who spend it anyhow to those who treat it with tender loving care and spend it thoughtfully.

If you want to be rich, do not think of what you can get. Think of what people need and how you can help them get it at a low cost.

No matter how wise he is, a broke man cannot teach you how to be a rich man. A wise pauper is only wise on paper.

When salary increases, do not buy a bigger car, instead, make bigger investments. Cars grow older, investments grow bigger.

Do not leave so much money in a bank, inflation devalues it. Invest in goods like real estate that increases in value as inflation hits.

Start a business. If you think you get rich working for someone, imagine how much richer the person is getting from your sweat.

As long as you develop your mind, you can be broke but never poor. If you do not develop it, you may have cash but still be poor.

When you sharpen a knife it cuts through objects faster. When you sharpen your mind, it cuts through problems faster. Read relevant books to sharpen your mind.

In a job you work for money, in your business money works for you. Even if you have a good job you're still a good hireling.

You are Christ's ambassador. Ambassadors do not suffer recession in a host nation. They are supplied by their home nation.

It is not a coincidence that KNOWLEDGE and IGNORANCE both have 9 letters and RICH and POOR both have 4 letters.

The biggest mistake many make is confusing laziness for faith. You cannot sit at home doing nothing and have faith to be rich.

Work on yourself and eventually people will work for you. Do not work on yourself and eventually you will work for other people.

If you do not know how to differentiate busyness from business you will end up delivering activity instead of delivering results.

You will not get rich overnight, but you will get rich over time if you set goals for yourself and work towards them. Goals give you something to aim at.

You do not get rich by making lots of money. You get rich by making investments. Money loses value. Investments gather value.

Keeping up with fashion can consume all your wealth but following up on your passion can create more of your wealth for you.

When you refuse to spend so you can invest your money they laugh at you. When the investment makes you rich they laugh for you.

To make money, find out what you love doing and do it, not because of money, but because you love it, then money will find you.

Do not depend on people who waste time. Time is the most valuable thing on earth. A person who can waste time WILL waste money.

For money to look for you, you must look for knowledge.

To prove that a business is far better than a job, consider that your kid cannot inherit your job but can inherit your business.

While faith is required for prayer to be answered, you also have a role to play. You cannot pray for a job then watch TV all day.

A bricklayer produces lots of brick, yet is poor because wealth has more to do with your mentality than your productivity.

A fool flaunts wealth by spending on material things that depreciate, but wise men spend wealth on people who can appreciate it.

Everybody has talents, but only those who develop talent can turn them to skills. People appreciate talents but pay for skills.

You know employees by their 'thank God it's Friday' attitude. You know entrepreneurs by their 'thank God it's Monday attitude'.

Do not work for money. Think for your money. Think of business ideas and get those who want to work for money to work your idea.

Before you take advice from anybody, look at their own lives. A man who has no money cannot teach you how to make money.

Do not be ashamed of getting your hands dirty while building your business. Dirty hands produce clean money.

Do not just work for your boss. Work on yourself. Read books and develop your talents and soon others will be working for you.

Money and wealth are external things. Your sense of self-worth is an internal thing. An external thing cannot fix internal issues.

When you are excited by anything you have the talent to do, do not turn it to a hobby. That is a big waste. Turn it to a business.

God did not give you talents so you find a job and earn salary. He gave them to you so you start a business and earn a fortune.

Rather than look for a job, look inside yourself. God gave us particular gifts that, if identified, could become your business.

The goal should be to be rich, not to look rich. Looking rich while you are poor will rob you of the capital needed to be rich.

Money is replaceable, time is not, therefore, a key to success is to be more meticulous with your time than you are with your money.

VI. COURTING, MARRIAGE AND RELATIONSHIP

Whoso findeth a wife findeth a good thing,
and obtaineth favour of the LORD.
PROVERBS 18:22

Those who rush to be the first to marry will be happy for a moment but those who wait to marry for true love are happy forever.

A man who buys a car for beauty and a man who marries a woman for her beauty alone will both upgrade to newer models when beauty fades.

Make sure you are marrying a woman whose 'I do' means 'I do', not 'I do as long as you have money and a position of power'.

Make sure you are marrying a man whose 'I do' means 'I do', not 'I do as long as you are beautiful and do not put on weight'.

Do not depend on your kid's teacher to teach him about real life. That is your job. Teach your kids how to handle money and life.

Loving parents do not just buy all kinds of gadgets and devices to amuse their kids. Loving parents spend quality time with them.

It is easy for women to call you honey when you have money. Wait for bitter times. If the love is still sweet, then it is genuine.

Sexy women are only attractive to men looking for sex. But VIRTUOUS and lovely women attract men looking for life partners.

A foolish wife expects her life to go well after cursing her man forgetting that a curse on him affects her since they are one.

The prayer of any man who looks after his girlfriend but ignores his poor parents is a prayer without effect 1st Timothy 5:8.

Some men confuse their wife or girlfriend with God. Calling your partner your all is not praise. It is stupidity. God is your all.

Dear young man, a man with a six packs is not as attractive in the eyes of an average woman as the man who earns six figures.

Excitement is not happiness and lust is not love. Marriage proposals made under influence of excitement or lust end in regret.

Ladies, before saying "I do", know what you are going to be doing. Know his temperament. Know his friends. Know his business.

A girl who sees a future with you will not let you spend all your cash on her but will urge you to invest for your future together.

Before marrying her, study her lifestyle. If it is expensive and she is not working, ask yourself if you are ready for such burden.

Guys, no matter how pretty a girl is, it is not worth it if you have to trade your peace of mind for a relationship with her.

While you are always on your phone, your parents are aging and your kids are growing. Put phone away and be present with family.

The biggest error a woman can make is marrying a man she has never provoked. Know how he acts during anger before saying I do.

Ladies, you attract men by the qualities you display, but you can only keep them through the qualities you actually possess.

The greatest gift you can give your family is not money, cars, houses, clothes or phones but your time and affection.

Ladies, a man who does not kneel down to God in prayer is never Mr. Right even if he publicly kneels down to propose to you.

Husband, if she was good before you married her and now you say she is bad, it must be her marriage to you that made her bad.

Loneliness is the worst reason to marry. If you do not like your company, how will your spouse enjoy it? Learn to love you first.

We cannot avoid loneliness by getting others to like us. We avoid it by liking ourselves.

Things not adding something tangible into your life are liabilities, not assets. A high maintenance girlfriend is a liability.

Always remember that a wife that can turn you against your parents can also turn your kids against you when the time is right.

Foolish men spend on women who give them their body and forget the woman from whose body they came. Honor your mother and father.

A handsome man who likes to dress well is only an asset to a woman if he also knows how to earn well, else he is a liability.

A marriage of two forgivers will last longer than a marriage of two lovers. If you cannot forgive, your love will turn to hate.

Dear dads, give your kids the present of your presence in their lives so they become adults whose lives are a present to yours.

Girls, a guy who gives you things is not necessarily generous. He may be investing and investors want a return on investment.

If you expect people to be perfect before loving them, your first casualty will be you. You are not perfect and so are others.

Do not use physical beauty alone to judge who becomes the love of your life or you may end up with the mistake of your life!

The reason it is called dating is because you are courting her to fix a date for the wedding not to fix a date to sleep with her.

Never leave a girl that is committed to you for one interested in you no matter how pretty. Interest shifts. Commitment does not.

Never be embarrassed by parents even if they are not polished because they were not embarrassed by you when they gave you birth.

Money pays for a wedding but not for love. Do not be fooled. If there is no love, you will have a good wedding and bad marriage.

Nothing can stop a man who has God at his front and his wife by his side. If it worked for Abraham, it will work for you!

Marriage is like taking tea. If your tea is not sweet, add sugar instead of throwing it away. Love is the sugar of marriage.

Providing for your family is the reason you wanted to be busy in the first place so do not prioritize business over them.

Dear single men, a man with high dreams, needs a wife with high vision not one with high maintenance.

www.ingramcontent.com/pod-product-compliance
Lightning Source LLC
Chambersburg PA
CBHW070618310726
48982CB00001B/118

* 9 7 8 0 9 9 8 1 8 2 9 4 0 *